The Martini of Destiny

Anthony St. Clair

rucksack *universe*

Rucksack Press
Eugene, Oregon

To Jodie, for all the adventures to come.

CONTENTS

"Just as all blood passes through the heart, all life, business and culture pass through Hong Kong. Since becoming an independent nation after The Blast, the city-state on China's southeastern seaboard has become renown as The World's Greatest City. It's easy to see why. From the inspiring drinks in the pubs, to the otherworldly weirdness of the concrete mythological figures in the Aw Boon Haw Gardens, the wonders are endless. All travelers will find new delights to marvel them, and new stories to bring home as souvenirs. After all, as the old saying goes, 'to tire of Hong Kong is to forget how to live the world.'"

— Guru Deep, *Hong Kong Through the Third Eye*

THE COFFEE
OF PERCEPTION

THE GLASS LOOKED LIKE a mountain inverted, a peak held in the hand. Jake Hongkong mixed the martini with the mastery of years, the gin, vermouth and glass all coming to the perfect cold temperature at his touch. In a blur he topped it off with the final ingredient, a few drops from the special black bottle in the unseeable cabinet behind a panel of the woodwork below the back liquor shelves. The drink looked and smelled the same, but for the man about to drink it, he did not know how different his life was going to become.

"I always heard you make the best drinks in

Hong Kong," said the man sitting at the bar. He hadn't noticed the special bottle. No one ever did.

"Only because I could never make it as a go-go dancer," Jake said as he finished preparing the martini. "My legs didn't look good in the tights." The man laughed, but in the back of Jake's mind he saw the black drops fall invisible into the glass, and the old tension rose again. "It's a shame you've never been in before," he said, straining the elixir into the inverted-mountain glass. He set the martini, the best he had ever made, on a cocktail napkin. I'm just doing my job, he thought.

"Figured it was time," said the man. "Today is going to be either the best or worst day of my life. I figured I might as well have the best drink of my life." The man raised the glass and sipped his martini. As the drink flowed through him, a smile brightened his face. He tipped the glass toward Jake. "That's the best damn martini I've ever had. There's hope for the world, so long as there are drinks as good as this."

"Anything to bolster a man about to face a difficult day. What's going to make it so hard on you?"

As the man's hand went to his jacket pocket, Jake could just make out a small rectangular outline. When the man opened the box, light glinted off a gold band, centered by a cloudy piece of green oval stone. "She hates diamonds, but she's a diamond of a lady."

All the right muscles tightened in Jake's face. "I bet she is."

"But jade, she loves that. So when it seemed like I needed to pop the question, this made more sense than the usual diamond nonsense."

"It's a nice ring, mate. Good on you."

The man sipped his martini. "And she's a nice girl. When the season's right."

"Nerves are understandable."

"It's not the nerves. She's like no other woman I've ever known. That woman burns with a fire that could keep all the world warm or burn it to a cinder. She's got a mind as brilliant as her body is beautiful. She's shown me kindnesses beyond my understanding, and anger I couldn't describe even if I wanted to."

"Sounds like one hell of a woman," Jake said.

"Thing of it is, I don't know if she wants to marry or not. Not just me, but anyone. Three years we've been going out, and sometimes when I look at her, I don't know if she's even really here. You ever know a woman like that? You look at her, and all you see is that she'd rather be somewhere else."

"I'm sure that's not a patch on you," Jake said. He looked around the bar, glad it was still empty. But he knew the quiet wouldn't last long. As the day wound down, he had little time before others would come in, seeking drink and needing something more. Hongkongers and expats alike soon would pack the pub—Chinese, Americans, the Brits descended from those who had stayed after The Blast destroyed what many had called a fledgling British Empire. Everything that had to happen, had to happen while it was just the two of them; he knew that as clearly as he remembered his real name. This man with the ring and the nerves needed not just the liquid courage in his glass, but some real courage that Jake would have to help him find in himself.

"Some women are so much their own person, they're so real, that it can just about hurt to look at them," Jake said. "They're more real, more here, than the rest of us. You meet a woman like that, you've met the most real person in all the world. There's no one like them, and it takes a real man to love them. A real man to bring out their love, to give them something safe, something they can open up to. It takes a strong man to love a strong woman."

"I don't know what chance I have." The man set down the half-full, half-empty martini.

"I'd say you have an excellent chance."

"Look at me," the man said. "I'm no great man. Average face, average build, average in all ways except how extremely average I am. I don't even know if I'll see her tonight. I don't know if I'll have the guts to call her, to ask her to meet me. I'm just a clerk in a gun shop. Hell, I grew up in New York, came to Hong Kong five years ago thinking I'd see the greatest city in the world, make it big. But all I am is here. I've got no prospects, no money. I've got nothing to offer her but myself. I have no destiny. No path. No goals. All I know is she and I should be together."

Jake set his hands on the bar and leaned down. The man's gaze flicked and trembled, but Jake looked in his eyes and saw the fear there, bloomed near to desperation. He's a man standing on the edge of the heart, Jake thought, a knife's edge of love or ruin. Even the destiny in his drink isn't quite enough—he needs more bolstering. "If she's the right woman to say yes, that's all she needs. You got this far. It's only a little farther to go. All you have to do is ask."

"And then what?"

Jake knew the real answer, but he also knew the right thing to say. "Then she decides."

"You couldn't have just said, 'she'll say yes?'"

"I could, but you know as well as I do that with a woman like that, even when you know you know the answer, the only real answer is that she'll decide for herself. And you'll love her, not anyway, not despite that, but because of it. You'll love her, you'll always love her, for being every bit and every moment exactly who she is."

The man used another sip as a moment to let Jake's words sink in. "Ever been married?" he asked.

"No time," Jake replied.

"Then aren't you just talking out your arse?"

Jake shrugged. "Never said I wasn't. When you get down to it, talking out of our arses is what every bartender does. We serve with one hand, take your money with the other and natter through our mouths to get you to the next round. When it comes to advice—and with bartenders, it always comes to advice, sooner or later—we talk out our arses. We have to, you see. Everything else is occupied. So yes, I'm talking out my arse. But I'll tell you this. I've poured a lot of drinks, I've listened to a lot of people tumble through their lives. The thing about being a bartender is you come to learn that you aren't just serving up drinks. You're serving decisions. Everyone has their moment. Everyone has their choices to make, their own destiny to set and follow. Over the years, it seems like people come in here to find their way. It's a tough job to have, tougher than it looks, but I love it. I've always loved it. People come to me, and they aren't just saying, 'give me a beer,' or, 'I need a martini.' What they're really saying, most of the time, is 'help me choose.' That's what I do. And for you, mate, I'm telling you: you have to ask her."

"You make it sound so important."

"Love. Choice. They're the most important things in the world, and they come out in the smallest of moments. You didn't just go out and snap up some off-the-shelf diamond because some ad told you to. You know her nearly as well as you know yourself. You listened to her for what she says and what she really says behind the words. You saw her for who she is. And you knew that a bit of jade on a band of gold was the best way to punctuate the most important question you'll ever ask. If you're man enough for that, then you're man enough for her."

The man downed the rest of the martini in one gulp. "Best damn martini I've ever had," he repeated. "And best damn advice I've ever gotten. You're one hell of a bartender, mister... What's your name?"

"Folks call me Jake."

"You say that as if it's not your name."

"It's what I go by. And yourself?"

"Declan," he said. "And that is definitely my name."

Jake smiled, stepped back and reached into his pocket. The man watched Jake roll a small, round, red and black stone from finger to finger in his right hand.

"Pretty cool rock," he said.

"I always carry it with me," Jake replied. "It reminds me of something important."

"I understand how that goes," Declan said, patting the ring box in his pocket, then taking out his wallet. "Okay, you've convinced me, but I know I better move fast, before the martini wears off. How much?"

Jake smiled. "This one's on me."

Declan laid some bills on the bar anyway. "For you, then. And... and thank you." He started walking toward the door.

"I'm sorry."

The words left Jake's mouth without his permission. I'm sorry I'm messing with your world, he thought. I'm sorry I'm messing with your destiny. And with hers.

Declan turned. Already it seemed the courage was melting out of him. "What?"

Jake looked around, wishing he could stare into himself to find out what had just happened. He grabbed the bills. "I'm sorry," he repeated, thinking fast, "but I just can't take these. Put them toward something later. Something for both of you."

Declan grinned, courage restored. "If you insist," he said, tucking the money back into his pocket.

"Good luck," Jake said to the closing door.

When the bar was empty again and the door had closed, Jake sighed, leaned back against the bar shelves and passed the round stone from finger to finger. He'd never dropped the stone, yet despite serving longer than any other Jake or Jade, he had nearly bungled this everyday task. All he had to do was bolster Declan's courage, get him brave enough to propose. "'He will ask, and she will answer,'" said the note that had been lying in the special cabinet when he came in. "'Then will come the question, and she will say yes.'"

But he'd recovered, and made good with what The Management had said he needed to do. Declan would go to her now, and he would ask his question.

The Management hadn't said what would happen next, but Jake had a sense of it now. A man like that, with such wavering confidence—he was someone who needed the stable I'm-here-for-you rock and the up-the-arse boot of a strong woman. She'd say yes. Liquid courage like what he'd just served... it had to be for love. He smiled. This kind of decision chased away the rest, all the hard ones, all the influencing and interfering that kept him awake at night: Getting two people to entwine in love made the whole rest of it worthwhile.

Jake turned away from the bar and its view of the pub, and instead examined the bottles on the shelves lining the back wall. In the mirror behind the bottles he glimpsed his reflection; his brown eyes glinted bright but muted, as if under a haze, like a lamp whose shade needed dusting. No gray wove through his short black hair. Beneath his white button-down shirt and his black trousers, his body still looked trim and felt strong—part of the benefits of the job, The Management had told him, just like the ability to serve any drink at the perfect temperature just by touching its glass or bottle. Sometimes it still seemed strange to him, the

Brazilian amongst so many Asians, but after all these years he had blended in as well as he could. Then again, no Jake or Jade ever really blended in. They just became a sort of invisible, known but not noted, vital but humdrum, like a traffic light or an artery.

He'd need to bring up more whiskey and vodka soon. The Deep's Special Lager would need changing before the evening was out. He'd put on a fresh keg of Galway Pradesh Stout when he'd arrived at the pub, but it seemed not nearly as full as it should have been. Jake made a mental note to hound their distributor about selling him a partial keg. Then he stooped and opened the real cabinet, unseeable and unopenable to anyone who wasn't a Jake or Jade. The bottles inside shimmered in the light of the pub, the light of the cabinet and some other light that Jake could never figure out. Five shimmering bottles, filled with five different liquids —Green #2, Gray #3, Brown #5, Silver #10 and Black #11. Like Jake, the bottles and their contents waited for the right moment. For the right need. For the right question.

They were there to answer.

"I'm just here to serve," said Jake. His gaze lingered on the small black bottle, barely big enough for a few shots. That wasn't usually there. Thinking back over his service, he'd hardly ever used Black #11. But Declan had needed a good dollop to get him on his way.

He was about to close the door when a rising thrum sound made him stop. The sound stopped too. Jake looked into the cabinet again. A new note had appeared.

Closing the cabinet and standing, Jake looked around the empty pub and opened the envelope. The typed sheet of paper always reminded him of telegrams, but something told him that wasn't exactly the way The Management sent their messages. The note read:

AN ANOMALY IN HONG KONG. NOT SEEN ANY BEING LIKE IT BEFORE. IT HAS VISITED EVERY PUB IN THE CITY, AND MAY BE COMING TO YOU. TRY TO IDENTIFY, OBSERVE AND LEARN ALL YOU CAN. IT IS AS A GHOST. — THE MANAGEMENT

After he'd read the note twice more, he let it go. The paper vanished before it reached the floor. It couldn't have been Declan, he thought. At least he had that figured. How was he supposed to keep an eye out for a ghost? Weren't they invisible? Or did The Management mean something else?

Jake took the stone back out of his pocket, rolled it between his fingers and looked out at the pub. The overhead can lights and candle-like electric wall sconces brought out the brightness of the mahogany tables, while leaving private shadows where drinkers could talk in seeming seclusion. The black walls weren't the usual standard-issue plaster white for the pubs The Management operated the world over, but they had told Jake that black was more fitting for Hong Kong. Jake had never asked why.

With every touch of stone to skin, of memory to remembrance, a growing, unidentified disquiet grew. His youth in Rio de Janeiro seemed further away than ever. After so long as a Jake, he had lived and worked not just a world but a lifetime away from his parents, and from the twins, so small when he was barely a man. He looked at the stone, smooth and crimson red, veined with jet. Yet he saw only the smiles on the twins' faces, so young then, when they gave him the stone. So proud to give it to their big brother. He loved them so deeply when he'd taken it, smiled big as the sun as he ruffled their hair. They started to say, "So you always think of us—"

Then his world had stopped. In that moment of love and purpose, The Management had come, and he chose and was chosen. He had been called, and he had decided to answer that call. Jake Hongkong, they named him. Hong Kong had never made sense, not even after all these years, but The Management weren't much for explaining. They had a world to keep turning.

Jake poured himself a cup of coffee and sipped it black. He never drank alcohol, since he never knew what he or a colleague might have done to it. And since coffee was the drink of ultimate perception, it couldn't be affected by anything any of them did anyway. But coffee was the first drink each Jake and Jade mastered. It helped them be alert of themselves and beyond. It helped them see and feel all the world and what they had to do while living in it yet apart from it. Jake remembered once asking why The Management didn't do coffee shops, instead of pubs. "You can always get coffee in a good pub," he'd been told, "but not the other way around."

No milk. No sugar. No booze. There was no correcting this cup of coffee, there was just the simple act of drinking. The coffee's warmth settled into his system. Jake felt his soul and his perception widening, deepening, reaching far beyond himself.

The earth itself moved over his tongue, from the wood fire of the coffee's roasted beans, to the purified water he used to make this one perfect cup. When he drank the last drop, not even a stray coffee ground stuck to the bottom. As Jake washed the mug, the world filtered through his senses. All the arguments and laughs, all the tender kisses and vicious kicks. A child cried; a woman sighed; a man spoke. Everywhere. All at once. They moved through him, the billions of people all over the world. Every person choosing, wishing to choose, wishing never to choose, feeling they could never choose, wishing they had chosen differently; he saw them all.

"Sometimes I wonder," he said. "Sometimes I don't know if I do the right thing. But my job is to help you do what you have to do. I hope you can forgive me."

In the corner of the pub, a shadow moved.

Dressed all in black, the man walked up to the counter, empty pint glass held in a gloved left hand. He must have been there the entire time, Jake realized. The only time he had seen the door open was when Declan left. The rush of the coffee fell out of Jake like gin from a dropped glass. An anomaly, the note had said. As a ghost.

"I'll forgive you," said the man, with an accent that seemed both Irish and everywhere, "long as you pull me another pint o' stout."

THE STOUT
OF REALITY

JAKE NEARLY DROPPED his stone, but he managed to get it back into his pocket. "You sure about that stout?" he asked. "I'm told I make a mean martini." A martini would be a big help, Jake thought, especially in figuring out how the hell you've been hiding out of sight all this time.

"Stout," said the man, smiling when Jake picked up a pint glass with a slight curvy bulge at its side. "And a proper Irish pint," said the man, nodding. "None o' that Yank sixteen-ounce crap." His accent refused to acknowledge the sound th, so "that" sounded more like "t'at."

"Each drink to its proper glass," Jake replied. "That's what I always say." *Do all ghosts know their beer glassware?* he thought as he started the 7-minute process that was a pour of Galway Pradesh Stout, or GPS. Blackest stout glinted with hints of red as the layers of beer foamed and settled, foamed and settled. "What brings you to Hong Kong?" he asked, looking at the man out of the corner of his eye.

"I guess you can tell from my accent that I'm not exactly from here," said the man.

"Ireland?" Jake replied.

The man nodded. "By way o' a few places, and I've been from a few other places too. But Ireland's dearest to me."

"All the more so, I'm sure, given how hard everyone there worked to recover from The Blast," Jake said. "Hard to imagine a stronger country, and with so much prosperity now."

The man said nothing for a moment. "Aye," he finally replied, a tremor in his voice. "I suppose the Irish made the best o' what a bloody mess they were served."

Mentioning The Blast unsettles him, Jake thought, looking at the man from the corner of his eye. The man's vague features said he was from anywhere, everywhere and nowhere. Looking at his face was like trying to grab an oiled window. One glance and Jake slid off to memories of walking through Rio de Janeiro. Another glance, and his mind saw statues of Buddhas in the city shrines, all topped with the money-green flag of the Independent City-Nation of Hong Kong. The only thing he could lock onto was the intense gaze of the man's brown-black eyes. They were like the nighttime sky, an ocean at midnight, brown rushing rivers, the bark of ancient trees and fresh-tilled vibrant black earth, all at once.

Dark as stout, he thought, second of the four drinks that no Jake or Jade, that not even The Management, could influence. Stout was too real to be anything other than what it was: reality in a glass.

"A man trying to suss out reality in his pint," Jake said. "Sounds to me like someone who came a long way to try to figure out a few things."

"Lot o' folk say Hong Kong is the Greatest City in the World."

Jake shrugged. "Bangkok and New York like to argue about that," he replied. "Even London seems to be trying to catch up, though Dublin gives as good as it gets. They all have plenty to offer. But Hong Kong offers something that no other city quite does."

"What's that?" the man asked.

"Answers," Jake replied, then grinned. "Though for every answer, we seem to have three questions."

"You could say I spend my life trying to

understand what motivates someone to an action," said the man. "What is destiny? What is decision? Do we have one or the other? Do we have either? Is there direction and purpose? Or are we just shunted along the oiled chutes o' our lives?"

"Tough questions," said Jake. "And Hong Kong would answer, 'yes.'"

"Hong Kong's a git," said the man with a chuckle. "But I suppose many would've said the same o' me at one time. I used to think I knew." The man's left hand clenched. "What would you answer?"

The pour was nearly done. Jake added a little more, then let the beer rest. "I would agree," Jake said. "I think we have the destiny we decide we're going to have, and we live the decisions we're destined to make."

"Sounds like a snake eating its own arse."

"That's life."

An inch of white foam topped the stout. Jake had heard it said that Arctic snow kept trying to be as white as the famous foam on a pint of GPS. Deep inside the layers of black beer, bubbles rose as the beer continued to settle. He looked straight at the man as he carried the pint over.

The glass nearly fell out of his hand. How had I not noticed before? he thought. It shouldn't be possible—but then again, a lot of things have happened the last few minutes that I wouldn't have thought possible.

He clenched the pint tighter, thinking fast. Even the dead still had one. But this man didn't.

When he was being trained, The Management had explained to Jake that destiny and decision were a double helix of existence, intertwined yet parallel, and as present in every person as the double helix of their DNA. They taught him to see the silvery chains that flowed from every being and object, to discern between the dimmer strands of potential action and the bright chain of the course that needed to be followed. The job of every Jake and every Jade was to bridge the two, at the right time, in the right place, for the right person. All around him the helix flowed, intertwining every person in the city, in the world.

Except for the man with the gloved left hand.

Where destiny and decision ran, this man ran parallel. No helix shone from him. He was separate, yet here. Of the world, yet apart from it.

Like a ghost.

"I'm impressed with your pour," said the man after his first large quaff left the glass a quarter empty. He laughed. "Destiny in a glass, a pint o' stout is. Opaque, slightly bitter and irresistible."

Reality in a glass, Jake thought. Stout was too real to be anything other than what it is: not just the reality, but a reminder of all that is. "Devout to stout, are you?" Jake asked. He sensed a need to hurry. Right now, the pub was empty of anyone but

Jake and the man, but customers were on the way. Jake could already hear the questions in their steps.

"I've drunk ol' GPS for many a year," said the man. "I was drinking Galway Pradesh Stout since before GPS had anything to do with bingity gadgets in science-fiction movies. You know, the ones that tell you where you are and where you're going." He laughed. "Gadgets telling you where you're going. Gads. It's as silly as those movies where people have phones in their pockets. Give me a pint o' stout any day. Tastes better, and it's far more accurate."

"You seem to know a lot about stout."

"As you seem to know a lot about martinis," said the man. "And their effects."

The Management had said the anomaly had been to every pub in Hong Kong, Jake thought. Was he looking for the city's Jake? He kept his voice even. "What, do you mean when someone has too many martinis?" Jake replied. "Always strikes me funny how many people suddenly think they're international spies."

The man laughed. "I mean the other effects," he said, taking a quaff of stout and staring at Jake.

"Hangovers?"

A corner of the man's mouth twitched. "I won't bandy with you," he said. "You're not the first one I've seen. I know it's not every bartender, but the ones like you do something different. You don't just serve the drink. I can see it with every pint."

"I'm just a bartender," Jake said evenly. He may see something, he thought, but not enough to know. He can't see me influence the drinks. But he already knows more than anyone should. Jake's thoughts went to the cabinet. Was The Management aware their ghost was here? Would they intervene?

No, he realized. They wouldn't. A man beyond destiny was a man beyond their influence.

"But you aren't just a bartender," said the man. "Look, there's many the person hunkers down before a drink. Gives their futility up to it, their desperation, almost like a sacrifice to some god. Like they're praying to saint rum and tonic—"

"You mean gin and tonic?" Jake asked. Without thinking about it, he took his rock out of his pocket and began twirling it between his fingers.

"That too," the man replied. "Got no time to keep up with fancy liquor drinks. But as I was saying. It's like they're praying to saint gin and bourbon for a bit o' help, a sense o' direction. And it provides. Usually it steers 'em right... though sometimes it leads 'em astray." The man glanced at his left hand; a wince crossed his face. "I've let a glass too many lead me to a fair mistake or two as well. That's why all I drink now is the stout. But you folk? I see you give a drink to someone. Next thing you know, it's like they know what to do. They see a way forward. Then they take hold o' it and run like feck before the alarms go off. And that's who you are. You show the way. You show the answers."

Jake said nothing, and the man smiled. "I thought so," he said, taking another swallow of stout.

"Okay," Jake said. "You said you came to Hong Kong seeking answers. May I ask you a question?"

The man nodded.

"What happened to your hand?"

For a moment the man said nothing. "A boring story concealed by a far more fascinating glove," he finally said. "But that pelican got as good as he gave." He glanced at Jake's fingers. "Nice bit o' rock," said the man, pint raised in his right hand. "I used to be able to do that trick too. Where'd you get that fine piece o' stone?"

"Same place you had it out with that pelican," Jake replied. "Here." He didn't know what made him do it, but something, some smugness in the man's face made Jake flick the stone through the air. The man's left hand shot up to grab it, but his fingers jerked, and the rock collided with his fingertips. The smug fell off the man's face. The stone clattered onto the bar, spinning on the polished wood before coming to a rest between the two men.

The man looked at his fingers, stretched like claws as he slowly lowered his arm. The left hand seemed so much smaller than the right, Jake realized.

"I made a big mistake once," said the man,

looking away from Jake and into his glass.

"We all make mistakes," said Jake, looking at the stone. "No matter what we do, sometimes all we wonder is what mistake we made once, which one we're making now, and which we'll make over and over."

The man chuckled. "Some mistakes are much bigger than others. Bigger than those who make them. Damn near bigger than the whole world." He drank the last of his stout, then looked Jake in the eye. "I'm looking for something I lost when I made my mistake. I'm trying to find my way back to it."

Jake looked from the man's face to the empty space above his head. He moved to pick up the stone, but a sound made him look away. The stone stayed on top of the bar. The door opened and the evening came in. "Excuse me," Jake said. In the new flurry of customers, drinks, decisions and destinies flew from Jake's fingers. After the rush he looked again at the barstool.

The man was gone.

Then ultimate reality crashed into Jake. The man hadn't paid for his pint. But not only that—Jake remembered the strangely empty GPS keg, and he realized where the stout had gone. Dammit, Jake thought. I just got ripped off by a ghost.

He reached into his pocket for his stone, but found nothing.

Wait, he thought. It was still on the bar when I

turned away. He looked, but only the empty glass sat there.

Jake checked the floor on both sides of the bar. Nothing.

And then he knew.

The two servers had just come on duty, and not a moment too soon. He waved one over. "Emergency. You're tending bar for a while."

"What? How long?"

Jake didn't answer, just sprinted for the door to chase a ghost. Until he could catch up to the man with the gloved left hand, destiny would have to get along without him.

THE ABSINTHE
OF DREAMS

JAKE RAN into a dream.

He'd pressed through the narrow side streets of Hong Kong's Wan Chai District in Causeway Bay. The man with the gloved left hand was far ahead, but still just barely visible. Jake dodged taxis, ran past the signs flashing in English and Chinese, and elbowed his way through the end-of-the-day crowds. The noisy world clanged like his pounding heart while he ran as fast as he could, but he couldn't catch the ghost.

Jake turned onto a climbing walkway of gray stone and gray walls, just as the man passed under a red and gold gate. When Jake passed through it, the world seemed to change. The city's glaring lights and endless cacophony faded, replaced by the bright colors of legends and hells.

The Tiger Balm Gardens, he thought, looking for where the man with the gloved left hand had gone. Built by Aw Boon Ha, a man who'd made a killing creating and selling an herbal balm, the Gardens were an everyman's vision of the afterlife. All around Jake, the ground sprouted painted concrete figures. Walls writhed with golden demons, souls and myths. A woman rode astride a water buffalo. A phoenix rose in flight.

A woman sipping absinthe in the pub had once explained to Jake how the world soon would look to her. "My dreams take the green stream out of my eyes," she had said. "They leave my mind, liberated. They blossom to the world, and they show that beneath the dirty, cracked, dusty, greasy skin of what we call life, the world shines silver and gold underneath."

The Gardens could have been her mind, Jake thought, contempt lending harshness to his thoughts. He didn't like absinthe, and he didn't like the Gardens. The painted concrete seemed to shimmer, and he could not tell real from dream. He looked down one long passage of bright red, textured like cave walls. Entwined in the rock, a blue dragon shone with all the fire and power of the stars. No audience attended the dragon in the empty stone plaza below it; only a small, round bushy tree humbled itself before the dragon's might. But before he rushed toward the plaza, a neighboring passage caught his eye. Near a statue of a pig walking, a shadow faded. Jake ran toward it. He heard footsteps walking on a stone staircase. Walking, thought Jake as he dashed. Like the bastard's just out for a leisurely stroll in the eighteen levels of Buddhist hell. At the bottom of the stone steps, he looked up.

Above him stretched the gray steps, which then entered the seven floors of the Tiger Pagoda, spear of heaven, the only white pagoda in the city. At the top of the stairs by a doorway, the man stood calm and serene. "See you at the top," he called down. Then he disappeared into the pagoda.

Anger blasted Jake's weariness, and he ran up the stairs, through the doorway and onto more stairs. Fury drove him, but it wavered as the climb continued. The seven flights of stairs might as well have been taking Jake to the sky. Somehow the climb didn't seem to match the height. Jake stopped for a moment, breathing hard with a hand braced on the wall.

The pagoda wasn't that tall, by Hong Kong standards, yet the stairs went on and on. The fury gave out, but Jake's feet kept going. The stone steps seemed to have softened, as if going to quicksand under his feet. He wanted to lay down. But I'm a Jake, he thought. I have to know who he is—

He stumbled. His hands and knees smacked a flat stone floor. No more steps, only a small covered chamber and a single doorway in one wall, ringed in a gold glint of afternoon sun.

Jake pushed himself to his feet and passed through the door. The seventh floor, he thought. The cooler air and bright sunlight revived him. Nothing between him and the sky anymore, Jake's soul lightened, and he breathed deeply as he wandered the round walkway at the top of the white pagoda. It's like looking down from the clouds, he thought.

There was nowhere to hide, and nowhere to go but down the stairs or over the edge. At every curve Jake expected to catch up to him, but the man was nowhere to be seen. Jake peered over the edge.

Passing through the Gardens below, he'd noticed the wavy lines in the rock that made every piece of concrete seem like it was shivering, screaming and praying. Up above, with details lost to the height and the harsh daylight, only the bright colors remained, like a secret world revealed.

"I know what you're thinking," Jake heard. "It's like someone took the lid off a chunk o' the world, and this was underneath. Not saying that's accurate, but it's an understandable suggestion."

The man with the gloved left hand stood a few

feet away.

Jake walked toward him. "You stole my rock. You didn't pay for your beer. And I think you had more than one pint."

"More accurately," said the man, "you never charged me."

"You ran out."

"I've never been charged for a stout in my life. Saw no evidence that was changing now."

"You regularly run out on bar tabs?" Jake asked.

"That was a long run for you," the man said. "You're clearly winded. Would you like a moment to ponder and rest?"

"No," said Jake. "I'd like you to pay what you owe. And I want my rock back."

The man took the rock out of his pocket and held it up. "Why do you want this back so badly?"

"Because it's mine," Jake replied.

"You sound like a six-year-old," the man said. "It's just a rock. What does it matter to you?"

"It was given to me by someone I love."

"A lover?"

"No. My little brother and sister. Twins." Jake walked toward the man.

"When did they give it to you?"

"Why are you asking?"

The man held the rock over the side of the pagoda. Jake stopped. The man said, "I'm asking because I understand how much it matters to you.

How much you would do to get it back. How it's yours and you can't stand that it's lost. And however much you want this rock, I can assure you, it's a pint in an ocean o' stout compared to how badly I want back what I've lost."

"And what did you lose?" said Jake.

"I lost my destiny," said the man. "Before you were born. Before these gardens were here. A long time ago. Ever since, I've been trying to find my way back to who I was. Who I am... who I should be. I don't know anymore. I'm in pieces, and the biggest piece missing is that it's like I'm blind. I used to be able to see so much before me, know where I needed to go and what I needed to do. Now it's like I can hardly see or know anything."

"Is that why you came looking for me?"

The man nodded. "You lot do something to people, help them choose, help them find their destiny. I figured there had to be something you could do."

Jake looked long at the man. His anger dissolved into pity. "I wish there were."

"There isn't?"

Jake shook his head. "There are things I do that help people find their way, I'll give you that. But I can do about as much to your life as I could a pint of stout."

"It's through the drinks, then?"

"Except for coffee, stout, absinthe and water.

Those four are immune to us. All I can do is pour them. Coffee opens people's eyes to existence. Stout is pure reality. Water accepts and enfolds everything. And then there's absinthe... absinthe is like this place, these Gardens, in a glass."

"You don't seem to care for it."

"It's the stuff of dreams, but not the real dreams," said Jake, bitter as the green drink he hated to serve. "It takes you to the stuff that isn't real, can't be real, shouldn't be real. It gives people fluffy pipe dreams, instead of showing them what they could do, if they just tried. I always find it too bitter to be real dreams."

"Some dreams are bitter," replied the man, staring down toward the Gardens, his left hand flexing. "I know that taste too well, and it never did me any good." He clenched his left hand. "Quite the opposite."

Jake looked at the man. "There's nothing I can do for you. If there were, I would. Not because you have my rock. Not because you could chuck it over the side and I'd lose the only memento I have of two of the people I love the most and will never see again. I'd do it simply because no one should have to feel as you do. And I'm so, so sorry that there isn't anything I can do for you. Whatever it'll take for you to regain your destiny, the only thing I can figure is that you have to find your own way."

The man looked away from the gardens to Jake.

A breeze was the only sound. "I'm sorry I took your rock," the man said at last. He held out his hand.

Jake walked forward, and the man let the stone fall into Jake's palm. "I can understand why you did," Jake replied. "You wanted me to understand. Maybe if I understood enough, I'd do what you wanted."

"I'd hoped. I've searched a long time. But I guess what you said is something. You can't help me."

"But maybe you can help yourself."

The man nodded, a small smile on his everywhere face.

"I have to say, though," Jake said, "how about you pay me what you owe?"

"Depends on what you're calling due," the man said, a resolution in his eyes. "I'm sure there's many as would say I owe them a lot." The man smiled. "Since you're offering me a bill for only a few pints, I'll settle up with you," he said, but he made no move to a pocket or wallet. He just nodded and stared at the plaza below. "You helped me understand. I'm going to do the same. Have a look down by the big blue dragon."

In the gardens, a man waited. He must have arrived while I climbed the stairs, Jake thought. The man stood between the round tree and the dragon wall. His inhales and exhales weren't air, but fear and courage, entwined and alternating. He paced around the tree, from the wall to the tree, and all around the plaza. But not once did he look back at the passageway. "Declan?" Jake asked. The man nodded.

"I don't understand why you want me to watch this," said Jake. "I already know how this will go. I helped make it happen."

"And what happens?" asked the man, his gaze still on Declan. "What do you think happens?"

"Declan's going to propose to his girlfriend. She's going to say yes."

"Aye," said the man, turning his gaze to Jake. "Declan's going to propose. She is going to say yes. But you only have the beginning and the end. We're here so you can see the middle."

The words of The Management's note flared into Jake's mind: "He will ask, and she will answer. Then will come the question, and she will say yes."

Below, a woman marched up. Seeing her from a height did nothing to diminish Declan's description of her. Arrows didn't fly as directly as she walked. The air about her seemed to shimmer with fire and comfort, the steel of the soul's truest hardest backbone. Yet underneath all her smoldering flames, soft questions never let themselves be answered.

"He didn't tell you this," said the man with the gloved left hand. "Her eyes are blue and gold, as if the sun could rise over the Mediterranean in noonday light."

"When have you seen her?" said Jake.

"You bartenders aren't the only ones who do a lot o' seeing and listening and knowing in this world," said the man. "But we aren't here to talk about her eyes. We're here to settle up." The man stood next to Jake, his hands curled over the pagoda railing, and he nodded toward the dragon wall. "Now watch," he said. "Here it comes."

Declan and the woman stood between tree and dragon. Declan took her hand. Jake couldn't hear the words, but all the same he knew what was being said. Nor could he see the expression on her face, but in the air, a hesitation hung.

Then the world stopped.

A bird had been flying by the top of the pagoda, level with Jake's head and only a few meters away. Now it hung in mid-air, wings up above its body. "What's going on?" Jake asked.

"Declan proposed," the man replied. "She's going to say yes. But here's the part you didn't know."

Below, three hooded figures appeared in a triangle around the pair. One wore cloaks and robes of blue and green. Another wore black and brown. Beneath the dragon, the third shimmered silver and gold. Jake's sharp breath was the only sound.

"I take it you know who they are," said the man.

"They're... they're The Management," replied Jake before he could stop himself.

"And what are they here for, Jake?"

Jake looked away.

"No," the man said. "You serve your drinks and you play with people's lives. If you accept what you do, then you also accept the results o' what you do. And you will bloody well watch them unfold. So I'll ask again, as you watch: what are they here for, Jake?"

The figures moved closer. Declan stood still as the blue dragon on the wall. But the woman turned, looking at each figure. She didn't run, Jake realized. He admired that. "I ran, when they came for me," he said. "They're here to make a proposal of their own."

"Is this how you blokes get made?"

"We call it 'chose and chosen,' but yes. They come for us. It's like we're called by something in existence itself, and yet it's also a decision we each make. There's a moment for each of us, where all these feelings churn inside. Love and adventure. Futility and hope. Future and destiny, choice and determination. Then the world stops. And they appear."

The man nodded. "Where did they come for you?"

The tenderness in his voice surprised Jake. He took the stone from his pocket and turned it in his fingers. "Where I grew up," Jake replied. "In Brazil. Rio de Janeiro. Just after my twin brother and sister gave me this. The day itself had been horrible. I'd been rejected from a bunch of jobs I applied for. I couldn't find money for university. I hated everything about me, everything around me. The world was desperation and futility. Then the twins came up to me, wet and muddy from playing at the river near where we lived." He held up the stone. "They gave me this. Said it was the only rock they'd ever seen like it, and they thought I should have it. That wherever I went and whatever I did, even if I was away from them, I could have this with me and always think of them, and they would be with me. I took the stone, and my frustration turned to love. I remembered all that was good about my family, about home. I thought things would be okay. I would figure something out."

"And then... they came for you."

Jake nodded. "All they do is ask. They explain what you can become. What you will do. They even explain how it all works. The pubs. The alcohols. How to all the world, we seem like any other bartenders. But what we really serve isn't drinks. It's decision and destiny."

"What if you had said no?"

"Then I would have had no memory of their appearance. The world would've clicked back into motion without a hitch, and I would have... I would have... I don't know what I would have done."

"What will she do?" the man asked.

Jake looked at the three hooded figures, now

standing around only the woman. The statue of Declan stood staring at them, yet saw nothing. Just like the twins had looked at him, all those years ago. They wouldn't remember, Jake thought, just as Declan wouldn't remember. But he would never forget.

Neither would she.

"She's going to become one o' you, isn't she?" the man asked. "Then the world will move again, that poor bastard is going to get his breath back, and he'll be standing alone below a dragon, ring held in his outstretched hand, and him feeling like the world's biggest eejit."

"I... I didn't know. I thought my job was to bring them together. Give him the confidence to get her to say yes."

"And you did your job," the man said. "She said yes. Just not to the question you expected."

Jake looked at Declan, at his outstretched hand, holding the ring of gold and jade. In his own hand, Jake twirled the stone from finger to finger. The bird hung in the air.

"I broke his heart," Jake said.

Wings rose and fell. The bird flew past the pagoda.

Jake's breath hitched. His fingers fumbled.

The stone fell.

Jake lunged for it, but the red and black stone plummeted away. It bounced off the railing below and fell toward the dragon plaza. The woman and The Management had just begun to fade when, Jake was sure, the stone's fall must have ended in clatters and bounces, spinning the way it used to do in Jake's fingers.

The figure in gold and silver looked up. Jake jumped back, hoping he hadn't been seen. After a moment, he peered over the edge again.

The four figures, The Management and the new Jade, had vanished.

"No," Jake said.

In the plaza below, Declan shook, startled. He realized he was alone—and holding out an engagement ring for a woman who wasn't there. A broken wail rang up the pagoda. "I don't know if they saw us, but we better get out of here," he said, turning to the man with the gloved left hand.

No answer. Jake looked around, and was alone.

THE WATER
OF ALL AND NOTHING

THE WORLD FADED to flashing neon and gray concrete as Jake snuck out of the Tiger Balm Gardens. The calm, sunny day had surrendered to stormy evening clouds, and a charge crackled the humid air.

Jake camouflaged himself in the crowded streets. Declan had run out of the gardens moments after the world began moving again, and Jake didn't want to run into him on the streets of Hong Kong. He tried to listen for Declan and for the man with the gloved left hand, his physical sense of hearing receding to his mind's stronger perceptions, honed by experience and The Management's training. But his jangled thoughts were too loud for his own head, and he could not focus enough to hear the lives and destinies around him. Every step Jake took, he waited for the strike—a hand on his shoulder that turned into a punch in the face from Declan, or a still world where suddenly he was penned in by the three beings of The Management. As for the man, he had vanished, and Jake had not caught so much as a glimpse.

One word dominated what little thought and conversation Jake could hear: storm. A gust of wind bullied the crowd. Arms flew over faces; people snatched at their newspapers; a startled man dropped his briefcase. Needles fell in an impersonation of raindrops. In moments, the storm bucketed down. Streets emptied. Jake and the storm wandered now. He stumbled past the flashing signs for noodle shops and news vendors, haircut-and-head-massage joints and nondescript bars. His own pub lay on the other side of existence. Despite the heat of the day, a chill soaked from Jake's clothes and deep into his body.

Water, Jake thought. The basic liquid of the universe. So powerful it can seem heartless, like a god who doesn't heed a prayer.

At an empty street corner he stood still, raised his head, closed his eyes and opened his mouth. Water can dissolve just about anything, he thought.

Water embraces anything, is within everything, yet it always stays itself.

I wish I could do that.

"We are to be like the four," The Management had once said in the training. "We are to see clearly. We are to hold reality. We are to realize dreams. But above all, we are to be like water: all destiny, all decision, all existence, flow through us. We are to hold all and nothing; we are to be ever-moving, ever-changing, as life changes, but we are to always be ourselves."

Jake remembered how he started nodding, when they said that. A warmth had spread through him, like a mother's touch, like a beloved's kiss, like a whisper of yes from a god. "This is how I will live my life," Jake had said. "This is who I am and who I always will be. I promise."

Rain stung his tongue, cheeks and eyelids. He lowered his head and looked around the shining, slick streets. "I'm not like you," he said to the rain. "I didn't want to let life just happen to people. I wanted to help... I thought I was helping. But we don't help. You wash the world clean. But not me. I rip people apart from their lives. And for what?"

The wind pushed him, and Jake started walking again. "What if I don't go back?" he asked the wind. "What if I just let you blow me around, and go wherever you take me?"

The wind didn't answer, but the rain fell harder

as Jake arrived at another corner. Across the street was the door to his pub. No, he thought, The Management's pub. I'm just the bartender. I just do what they tell me to do. And what else could I do anyway?

He was who he was, and that had made him who he was: a Jake, chose and chosen. "That's all I am," he said as he crossed the street. "A nothing who does what he's told." His shoes squished as he opened the door.

Every chair, every bar stool, every bit of floorspace was packed with rump or feet. And in every murmur, every chat, Jake heard the regrets of people who wished they'd had a raincoat, or at the least an umbrella. He envied their regrets.

Drops beat like flung nails on the picture windows at the front of the pub. Behind the bar, he grabbed some towels and dried himself off as best he could. The heat of so many people brought a wet warmth to the air in the pub, but a clamminess had wrapped itself around Jake's skin, and the towels couldn't scrub it away.

"It's about time," said the server he'd left in charge.

Jake nearly apologized, but only shrugged. "Had to be done. Thanks. Umm, take a break."

"Sure," she said, "because that's exactly what we need out here right now, is less people." She rolled her eyes, grabbed her tray and went back out to the floor, soon lost in a sea of glasses, lemon wedges, beer foam, business suits, dresses, and endless endless talk.

Except for being sopping wet, the world seemed normal again. Jake stood behind the bar and looked out around the pub. So many people—and so many soon needing not just another round, but a nudge.

A nudge.

To be behind the bar meant to do it all again. To bring about heartbreak and separation. But what else had he wrought over all these years? Destiny, decision—but at what price?

A woman came up to the bar, her eyes hard and glaring. Jake knew immediately what she needed—a drop of forgiveness for herself and the friend she'd had a falling-out with. The world outside had been black and empty, but here, he knew this. His body and his being slipped into the rhythm of what they knew, of who he was. The world flowed through him, and he kept none for himself. Could I stop doing this? he thought. No. I am a Jake. Destiny is my job, and this job was both my destiny and my decision.

He began pouring drinks, and as his body dried the world seemed to become clearer again. He had done what he had been instructed to do. He influenced; it was not his place to question or doubt. What happened to Declan was unfortunate, but necessary; her destiny was bigger than any ring he ever could have offered her. Just let it go, Jake told himself. Just let it wash away in the rain. He looked at the people in the pub, at all the shining helixes flowing from them, intertwining with other people's, intertwining with the unknown path the world moved along.

This is my world, Jake thought. And I still have work to do.

At least he'd learned more about The Management's ghost. He'd have to figure out how to tell them what he knew...

Jake started to take another order. Then the first screams made him look instead toward the pub door.

Rain poured off the man's clothes, as if fleeing his fury. The crowd in the pub shrank away, leaving him in his own world, clear space all around him.

Then the rage in his eyes found Jake, and Declan raised the gun.

THE MARTINI
OF DESTINY

JAKE RAISED his hands. "We can talk about this," he said. "But it's just between you and me. Can we agree on that?"

Declan smirked. "I don't think we'll agree on much right now, Jake."

"At least send the people away. They have nothing to do with this."

"They have everything to do with this, and they need to stay," Declan replied. "They need to understand. They need to see."

"See what?"

"What you do." Declan waved the gun from Jake,

pointing at the bar. "What you really do." Declan turned and looked at the frightened crowd. "You come into a pub for a drink. Nothing out of the ordinary. But when you come in, there's something nagging at you. You don't quite know what to do with your life. You have a drink or two, mixed by my fine friend here. But when you leave, something about you has changed. Now you know what you want to do. Where to go. What direction your life needs to take. Have you ever noticed that?"

A few people nodded.

"Don't you ever wonder why? This man... he does something to us. I think we have a right to know what that is."

Jake felt the eyes bore into him. One man's face had an angry redness to it; Jake remembered the gin and tonic that had led the man to confront his parents about being gay. A few people away, Jake thought of the glass of red wine that a woman had used to leave her job. She didn't look happy either. They're curious, he thought, but also angry. Intrigued, and on a simmer. They think life is fate, or they think life is choice. They want to know which is which. "I'm just a bartender, mate," he said.

Declan turned back to face him. "Then why were you there when she broke my heart?"

Jake's shoulders slumped.

"One moment she was there. The next she was gone." Declan reached his other hand into his pocket, and held up a small, round, black and red stone. "But your rock, your stupid little rock, was clattering around my feet. Like it had been thrown at me." Declan waved the gun as he turned in place, in a jaunty broken circle. "Like it had been thrown at me," he repeated. "I thought no one else was there. But you were there. Where were you?"

"I wasn't—"

The black end of the barrel seemed blacker when it was pointed directly at you, Jake thought.

"You were!" Declan shouted, the gun barrel steady, so steady. "You were there! Now say it. Say it!"

Jake nodded. "I was there."

"How did you even know?"

"You... you told me earlier."

Declan shook his head. "You're a rotten liar, Jake the bartender. But I know there's one way you tell the truth better than anyone." He nodded toward the bottles behind Jake. "Make me a martini." He smirked. "Make it two."

"Two?"

"Yes," Declan said. "One for me, as you made it earlier. And then another, exactly the same. For you."

Jake nodded. He can't see me approach the cabinet, he thought. It's okay. I can influence his, and not mine. Jake stopped, his hand hovering a moment at the martini glasses. But wait—I don't know which one he'll drink. I could just as easily wind up with the wrong martini. I'll have to influence both of them, or not do it at all.

"What's wrong?" Declan asked. "It's okay, Jake. The whole pub and I are watching your flawless technique."

Jake thought fast. "How do I know you aren't going to hurt these people? You keep waving that gun around. You're mad at me, fine. But what right do you have to put their lives at risk?"

"What right did you have to take her away?" Declan said. "But I'm not going to shoot them. Any bullets come out of this gun, they have your name on them. But here, I'll set your mind at ease." Declan nodded at four women around a table. "Mind if I take this table?" he said. The women moved away, and Declan sat down, his back to the door, facing Jake. Declan set down the gun. "There," he said. "That should make you feel better." He rested his hand next to the handle. "But any funny business, any grabs for a shotgun or bat or phone, and you'll wonder where the holes came from."

Jake sighed and took down two glasses, lightly chilled despite the heat in the room, or maybe that was just how cold he felt. It was too risky to influence either drink. He didn't even know what happened to a Jake or Jade who was influenced. Did it work the same way? Did it throw a wrench into the works of destiny? The gazes and souls in the pub pressed at him, nipped like fish in a river. They must think Declan's a lunatic, he thought. And if he is, is that my fault too?

The gin flowed like time and destiny, clear as pure rivers. The splashes in the glasses seemed to sigh, as resigned as Jake was to what was happening. He dashed one part dry white vermouth to five parts of gin. Then he nodded toward Italy and France, the way he'd been trained. "We get better pricing that way," The Management had explained. Jake wondered why those old memories were even in his brain right now. Maybe because he feared he wouldn't be creating new ones?

Gin and vermouth breathed in the glass, colder, clearer and more honest than any crystal ball.

Jake brought the drinks to the table, set one in front of Declan, one in front of an empty chair. Declan nodded, and Jake sat down.

"What do you think this will accomplish?" Jake asked.

"They'll know what you do," Declan said. "You mess with people, Jake the bartender. I don't know exactly how, but you do. And we're going to show them how. We're going to show them that every time you serve someone a drink, you're messing with their lives, the way you messed with mine."

"I didn't mess with your life," Jake said. "I served you a drink. The rest was you."

Declan smiled. "But as I was leaving, you also

said you were sorry. The whole time I walked toward the gardens, I wondered why you said that. I understand now, though. It's because you knew. It's because you set me up to be brave, decisive, to show her all the love I had for her. And the whole time, you knew she was going to say no." One hand next to the gun, Declan raised his glass and motioned for Jake to do the same. "Now quit nattering at me, Jake the bartender, and drink what you serve."

The glass warmed in Jake's hand. Declan's eyes glowed with anger, but beneath that glare Jake could see the glaze of exhaustion and pain. "To your health," Declan said.

The men sipped. Declan grimaced. "This isn't the same," he said. "Not the same at all." All around the pub, people grumbled. Low whispers fell like rain.

All the right muscles in Jake's face tightened. Even if you lost, he thought, you can't show that you lost. "You saw me do it before, and you saw me do it now," Jake said, measuring each word. "Same ingredients. Same proportions. It's the same drink."

"No," Declan said. "It's not the same. You left something out."

"It's the same—"

"Maybe the gin and vermouth. But not the something else. When I was in here earlier, that martini was different. One moment I felt scared and couldn't make up my mind what to do. One sip of that martini, and everything began changing. It was like the world had been bleary, but it was coming into focus. By the time I finished the drink, I knew my course. I knew my decision. It was like I knew my destiny. Only I didn't. You already know that though, just as you know what you left out." Declan pointed the gun at Jake. "I said to make these exactly like the ones before. Now whatever that was, put it back in. So everyone can see."

Jake hesitated, but Declan rested his thumb on the pistol's hammer. Jake saw a chance. "What's the use in threatening to shoot me? If you shoot me, you'll never get the drink. You'll never know."

Declan shrugged. "It's just an option. You took away my future. What do I care about yours?"

Jake opened his mouth, but there was nothing to say to the hard look in Declan's eyes. He took the martinis back to the bar instead, staring at the unseen cabinet, his back to Declan and the people trapped in the pub. Hundreds of eyes stared with him, but the gaze he felt most was the black eye of the pistol barrel.

Before him, the helix flowed brighter than ever. Maybe because it's mine? he thought. Different paths, different decisions, and from each one followed so many resulting actions and sequences. He saw himself shaking his head, saying he didn't know what he had done differently, but that it was the same drink. Something dark at the end of that made him shudder. The people in the pub seemed to simmer, and their looks all were hot with growing anger. In another path Jake opened the cabinet, and everyone saw what was inside—and from there, the world ran red, dim and then done. He looked through all the helixes, following each potentiality. Black and red, black and red. The crowd's anger burst the pub, and grew until it consumed the world like flame. No silver shining hope. No thread of a chance, no million to one odds.

"We help keep the world turning," The Management had explained once. "But to do that requires utmost secrecy. People would never understand that we don't throw dice, and we don't load the dice. We just give a nudge, to help them toward the paths they most need to take anyway. But the price is no one ever knowing about us or about you. If people learned about the Jakes and Jades, not even we know when the blood would stop flowing and the fires would stop burning."

Utmost secrecy, Jake thought. I understand. No one could know about the Jakes and Jades. No matter the sacrifice.

He turned around and faced the black eye of the pistol. "It was the same drink," he said. "I don't know what you think was so different. I could try to show you, but you know as well as I do that it was what it was."

Declan shook his head. "You're lying. I know you're lying. Why were you staring at the paneling? What's there?"

Jake controlled his face as best he could. "Something to stare at for a moment, while I thought things over. But there's nothing different for me to do. If you don't like it, shoot me." Jake stood behind the martinis, his arms by his sides, hands palm out, raised, open.

"I will shoot you. Add the last ingredient, dammit," said Declan. He steadied his pistol arm.

"Go ahead," said Jake. "You don't care about my future? Fine. But before you pull that trigger, let me have my last words, at least." Declan hesitated, and Jake threw his hope onto the path that stemmed from that pause. "I cared about your future, Declan. I cared about your future more than I can say. More than you will ever know. And no matter how many times you shoot me, no matter what else you do, know this first: down as deep as my soul goes, I thought—I believed—I knew that she was going to say yes. And I was wrong too."

The grumbling in the crowd lessened, and the anger seemed to cool.

Declan stepped forward, the gun level with Jake's head. "You bastard," he said, with a crack in his voice. "Add what's missing. Do it."

"Or what?"

"You know what!"

Jake stared deep into Declan's eyes. The helix flowed down the path he had chosen. "Think no one's ever tried to hold up this place before?" Jake said. "I've been a bartender a long time. People who really mean to shoot you don't keep reminding you. They just shoot you."

Declan stiffened his arm and tightened his finger on the trigger.

Jake closed his eyes. I've done my duty, he thought. Protected us as best I could. He breathed out slowly. The helix approached its black, dark, fading end.

But the shot never came.

"You thought she'd say yes?" Declan asked.

Jake opened his eyes. He nodded, staring at Declan as both men stood completely still. It didn't make sense, Jake thought—the helix ran black—but maybe it was The Management interceding? I'll take the chance, Jake thought. Talk Declan down. Get him out of the pub. Then The Management can take over and work on Declan's mind, remove his suspicions about the pub, about Jake, about what had happened to him. Jake wondered if Declan would wind up even remembering having a girlfriend, much less that she rejected his proposal. He couldn't see that part of the path; it was all blurry now, past the clarity of his choice, of the gun, of the moment's sigh of relief that the secret remained just that.

Then a martini glass exploded. Jake looked down. The pistol bounced off the bar and smacked his belly. Glass shards pierced his shirt and cut him. The crowd's paralysis broke. People ran for the pub door.

When the yell slapped his mind, he looked up too late. Something small and hard whacked him between the eyes and clattered on the bar top. The surprise made Jake step back, and he lost his balance. Declan was already leaping over the bar. The force of the man's weight knocked Jake into the shelves and against the wood paneling. His arm smacked a shelf. Bottles rained off the wall. The sharp scent of alcohol stung Jake's nose. Glass shards dug into his legs. Declan's punch swung him around, and his knee hit the paneling—no! Jake thought, not there!—but he stumbled. His feet slipped in a puddle and went out from under him.

As he fell, the hidden cabinet opened. The back of his head smacked the wooden pub floor. As Jake's world darkened, the special bottle of Black #11 tumbled out of the cabinet. He kicked up a foot, shutting the cabinet door again—Declan can't open it, only we can, he thought, only if we will it, but it's too late I have to—

Too much dark around the world, Jake thought, too much silence. I can't move all of a sudden. Declan kneeled down. In one hand he picked up the pistol. In the other, he picked up the black bottle, then stood.

"This is it," he said, "isn't it? Too bad everyone left. I really wanted an audience."

Jake tried to get up, but Declan set his foot on Jake's chest and pressed. "I thought so," Declan said. "I knew there was something else." He held the bottle close to his eyes. "How could something so small do so much to one man's world?"

On the bar next to glass shards and puddled gin, the other martini waited. Declan took the cap off the small bottle. "What is it?" Declan asked. "What is this, that you put it in my drink earlier, but not now?"

The fog in Jake's head stopped him from stopping himself. "Destiny," he heard himself say, his head lolling side to side. "Destiny."

Declan upended the bottle into the glass. Though thick black liquid poured in, the drink stayed clear and the glass seemed no fuller than before. He set the empty bottle on the counter and raised the martini, tipping it to Jake. "Then here's to destiny," Declan said, and he drank the entire martini.

"Too much!" Jake wheezed, but Declan had already swallowed. For a moment Jake thought everything would be okay.

Declan's eyes widened and he lurched forward, sucking in air that didn't seem to want to go into his lungs.

Jake's world popped back into focus. One by one, where helixes had flowed from Declan, the silvery chains began to blacken and wither.

"What's happening?" Declan asked, the words barely squeezing out of him.

The chains fell away, rotting to black and then nothing. Around Declan, the world shimmered, as if all of existence was cutting him out of the world, as if to protect itself.

"You drank destiny," Jake said. "Too much. And now... now your destiny is gone." Like the man with the gloved left hand, he thought. Two anomalies. Two ghosts.

"I... I don't have a destiny?"

"Not anymore."

Declan doubled over and then straightened back up, as if pulled by strings. He inhaled deeply, then exhaled. His eyes widened, and his body seemed to loosen and relax. The laugh that clattered out of him chilled Jake.

"Free... I'm free... you damned me... but you freed me too. All these years I've felt so lost and directionless. I always thought it was a fault in my character, in my soul. But now I understand. It's my liberation. There is no path but me, and no destiny but what I blaze. All the world is before me, and all my life is to do as I will." Declan laughed and laughed, all the while shaking and doubling over. His limbs jerked as he straightened up again. For a moment he calmed, his breathing less ragged, his body still. "Maybe you're all right after all, Jake the bartender." He looked Jake in the eye, and the breath nearly went out of Jake again.

Declan's eyes blazed red. Then the last of his destinies, the last of his possibilities, burned away and faded to nothing. His eyes dulled from red to black, black as the sky after lightning, black as the void after all the stars had burned out.

Declan smiled. "I'm going to like this."

Then he screamed, head back, every tendon so taut Jake thought they would snap like overburdened cables.

The glass fell from Declan's hand, and then the pistol fell. The scream stopped.

The pistol bounced off the floor. A bang shattered something. Jake's body tensed and contorted. A bottle must have broken, he thought. I'm drenched.

Declan's eyes widened when he looked at Jake. "No!" he said. "That's not... that's not what I chose. I'm sorry... I'm sorry..." Then he ran.

Jake heard the pub door shut as his sight went red. It kept darkening, first to gray, then to a deeper and deeper black. I need to clean up this mess, he thought. Why can't I get up?

The world kept getting darker. And then it seemed to stop.

CLOSING TIME

Jake woke in silence and pain.

The pub seemed dim, and the lights above him were different. To either side should have been the bar, and the paneling with the secret cabinet. Confusion fought with the throbs in his head, arm and torso. Then he saw the brass foot rail. I'm in front of the bar, he thought, not behind it.

It was still hard to see, and he dabbed a finger at his forehead, between his eyes. The cut there still oozed, but the blood seemed to be thickening. He remembered something hard and small smacking into his head.

His vision slowly brightened, and Jake sat up

amongst empty tables.

Pain cracked through his ribs. His breath fell out of him, and he couldn't even yell. I want to lie back down, he thought. It was getting to be so peaceful there, until I woke up... But then again, that's the problem.

He stayed sitting up, and he looked down at his side, at the brown-red stain around the hole in his white shirt. The hole in me, he thought. At least blood's not pouring out of my side anymore. Is that good or bad?

He looked up to see who else was there, but there was only him.

Then he noticed the hovering.

No one human, at least.

The three hooded figures of The Management floated. By his left shoulder was the figure in brown and black, and by his right shoulder hovered the figure in blue and green. And at his feet, in mid-air, was the figure in gold and silver.

"Jake Hongkong," they said in unison.

"Am I dead?" he asked.

The figure in gold and silver replied, "Not while we are with you."

He nodded. "But once you start the world turning for me again..."

No one finished his words.

Jake choked back the throbbing in his arm from where it had hit the shelf. Blood coated his forearm.

Dots of blood on the front of his shirt, combined with the little stabbing pains in his torso, made him wonder how much glass had peppered his belly. He wobbled to his feet.

"You should not stand, Jake Hongkong," said the figure in brown and black.

"Might as well die on my feet," he replied. "You can't save me, can you?"

"No," The Management replied.

"If you could," Jake asked, looking at each of them in turn, "would you?"

"No."

Jake nodded. "Not destined and all that, right?"

"We only help the world and all things follow their paths," said the figure in gold and silver. "It is not for us to make the path. We encourage and we influence. But we do not choose for others, or for ourselves."

"And all goes according to plan." Pain shot through Jake's side. He touched his hand to the wound. When he held up his palm, the fresh red blood looked far brighter and more alive than he felt. "Even this?" he asked.

"No," said The Management. There even seemed to be sadness in their voices. Or voice. He never knew if they spoke in harmony with three distinct voices, or if somehow the three beings used one voice between them. "This was not part of the path."

"Then what happened?"

"The path changed."

The pub seemed to spin. Jake nearly fell, but he forced himself to stay on his feet. "This is all because of your damn ghost."

"You saw him?" asked the figure in brown and black.

"He tricked me out of the pub."

"You left your post?"

"He stole something precious to me," Jake said. "Plus he didn't pay for his pints. Don't you know this already?"

The Management said nothing, until at last the figure in gold and silver said, "Where the ghost goes, we see nothing. We can only detect him by where he has been and what he has done, not by where he is or what he does."

"You're blind to him?"

"Yes. Please, Jake Hongkong, tell us what happened with the ghost."

Jake explained quickly, from the conversation with the ghost to the chase to the Gardens. For a moment he considered not telling them what he had seen. But a dead man might as well have a clear conscience, he thought. "And now we're here," he finished. "Declan drank the entire bottle of Black #11, and I'm about to die."

"We came as soon as we knew you were injured. The bullet tore an artery."

Pain ripped through Jake's torso, and he put a hand over the gunshot wound. "Too bad your little alert system couldn't just go off at 'threatened.'" He chuckled. "Do we have a suggestion box? I'd like to submit an idea. And what about all the people?"

"The people who saw, we modified their memories of their time here," said The Management. "They do not remember."

Surprise cut through the pain for a moment. "That's good news. All of them?"

The Management said nothing, and Jake saw the catch. "What about Declan?"

"The new ghost fled."

"But surely you can find him," Jake said, but stopped himself. "Wait. You're blind to him too, aren't you?"

Silence answered.

"I hope she's worth it," Jake said.

"What do you mean?"

"The new Jade," he replied. "I think that's what brought your ghost here. He had some hint of her destiny. Don't ask me how. But he's looking for his own lost destiny, he told me, and he believed we could help him find it."

"You should not have come to the Initiation," said the figure in gold and silver.

"Well, as you said, run-ins with your ghost apparently throw destiny off its tracks, and make decision not sure what to do with itself."

"You chased a ghost. You chased a man who doesn't exist anymore."

"Tell that to the stout keg," Jake said, anger rising up hotter than the dull pains. "Wasn't a ghost that drank half the beer in there. And it wasn't a ghost who led me to where you were going to be. Why aren't you asking yourself how he knew?"

"Because we knew too little and could only suppose," said the figure in blue and green. "There is much you have learned about the anomaly, and you have confirmed our suspicions."

"At least tell me what all I'm dying for," Jake said. "I've earned that much."

The Management said nothing. *I can't believe this*, Jake thought. *I'll be lucky if I live through the explanation—can't they give me that much?*

Then the figure in gold and silver spoke. "The anomaly, the ghost you chased, was once known as Faddah Rucksack. He was thought to have died in The Blast."

"But that was long ago, far longer than he could have been alive."

"Rucksack is not human, in the sense that you are generally familiar with."

"Clearly," Jake said, a touch of sarcasm offsetting how hard it was to keep his knees from buckling.

"While he's not dead, The Blast harmed him," said The Management. "It severed him from the world's destinies. And, most importantly, from his own destiny."

"And he's trying to find his way back. He told me this already."

"You did him a great service, Jake Hongkong."

"Some reward I'm getting." Jake sat down. Standing was really hard work. So was breathing, he noticed. It kept feeling less and less worth the trouble. "The new Jade." Bitterness and blood rose in Jake's mouth. "What's so special about her?"

For a moment, The Management said nothing. "She is not just another Jade," said the figure in gold and silver at last. "She will be the greatest of you all, and her destiny rises higher than we can see."

"Is that what messed things up for me?" Jake asked. "She lived in Hong Kong, and I'm the Jake of Hong Kong?"

"No," said the figure in blue and green. "It was the other. After he drank destiny, his actions were beyond us."

"The affected man, this Declan, is removed from our influence," added the figure in brown and black. "He is his own destiny now."

"And I guess I'm about to be removed from life," Jake said, shaking his head. Something warm and wet was on his cheeks. "I did what I could," he said. "I served. I listened. I influenced. And the world's still going."

"Yes," said The Management.

"What now?"

"Hold out your hand." The figure in gold and silver knelt down in front of Jake and stretched out its cloaked arm. Jake's stone landed warm in his palm. A smear of blood covered one edge. "Sometimes I hate what we do," he confessed. "We mess with people's lives."

"We keep the world turning," said the figure in blue and green.

"We manipulate," said Jake, "and you're just a bunch of heartless beings who tell humans what to do."

"We love life and living more than you can imagine," said the figure in brown and black.

"We see the alternatives," added the figure in gold and silver. "This is far preferable."

"Forgive me if I disagree."

The figure in gold and silver stood and said, "Jake Hongkong, we will show you. You helped a man who needs helping, and your heart believed. You did what you could. That, ultimately, is all we do—even us. Declan is now a man without a path, and a man with no destiny throws the world awry. Even we cannot see all that may come of this. Yet you also helped Rucksack, and the ramifications of that could be crucial to the fate of many. Maybe of us all."

In the corners of his eyes, Jake saw the other two figures moving forward, penning him in.

"You love life and living, you say?" Coughing stopped the rest of his words. Blood spattered onto the chest of his shirt. "Me too. Guess you can't always get what you want." He clenched the rock tightly. "I'd always hoped to see them again," he said. "The twins. Maybe even Mom and Dad. When I retired. Assuming they'd be alive. But I guess that wasn't my path. Not like you didn't know that already." He coughed again. Blood coated his mouth. He kissed the rock. "Fellas," he said, "business is done. I've done what I can for you. If I've got to die, what do you say we get on with it?"

"As you wish, Jake Hongkong."

The world flickered. Jake expected to be alone in the pub, but The Management remained around him. "Are we... back in the world?"

"Yes."

"You're still here?"

"We cannot stop you from dying, Jake," said The Management. "But we do not have to let you die alone."

The Management stretched their arms out from their sides. A low hum filled the room. Deep inside Jake, a flickering light started getting brighter. The light flowed up from inside Jake, through his body and beyond. It brightened the helix that was the only path left to him, now nearly at its black end, beyond which he couldn't see. The blood didn't seem as thick in his mouth anymore.

The Management made no sounds. They faded as the light got brighter and brighter. Then the light seemed to speak, and Jake followed its voice.

He wondered what it would be like.

Would his family recognize him?

The world flashed, and the pub was gone. He seemed to be moving, as if up a river, as if over mountains. Jake's body felt indistinct and far away, yet close as ever. He saw the paths before him, the different lights and darknesses. Then—were those smiles over there, and the smell of river mud? His sight adjusted to the bright light. Mid-day light. Mid-day sun. The smell of the river was everywhere.

He saw them.

They walked together, his mother and father in the middle, with the twins on either side of them. "Son," he heard, and, "Brother."

As he raised his arms, his hands opened and the stone fell. He didn't see where it went, and he didn't pick it up.

The world kept getting brighter and brighter, and they kept getting closer and closer. Then there were hands, and kisses, and hugs, and words he thought he would never get to say or hear.

The bright world blazed in a flash of white, and then all went dark again. When the lights flickered back on, the pub was empty except for the shadows, and except for the red and black stone clattering on the floor.

From the back corner of the pub, a man walked out of the darkness and shadow, an empty pint glass in his gloved left hand. He picked up the rock, stared at it a moment as if finding a long-lost friend, and put it in his pocket. The light glinted off his brown-black eyes as he walked behind the bar and drew a pint of Galway Pradesh Stout.

He took a long quaff. "Well," said Faddah Rucksack, "that explains a lot."

THANK YOU FOR READING!

Please tell your friends about this story and review it at your favorite bookstore. Reviews are the best way readers discover great new books, and I would truly appreciate it. Even a couple of sentences is a big help. Here's a list of stores:

anthonystclair.com/martini

MORE FROM THE RUCKSACK UNIVERSE

Home Sweet Road
anthonystclair.com/homesweetroad

Forever the Road
anthonystclair.com/forevertheroad

SUBSCRIBE TODAY

New story announcements, events, exclusive bonuses and more. Join the free email list:

anthonystclair.com/subscribe

Endless gratitude to the patient and adventurous souls who have been there for me on this journey...

Sean Keener for your motivation, optimism and for continuing to help me find opportunity while keeping it real, and to the BootsnAll Travel Network for the memories and ongoing inspiration to travel the world. Choya Renata, Robin Clemen, Jeanette Muscat, Stephanie Russell, Carla Brindle and Matilda Ertz for your attentive minds, astute feedback and amazing friendship. Willamette Writers for such a supportive community of writers and authors. Bonnie Donaghy for the awesome cover design. Readers no doubt will be relieved I refrained from using Photoshop. Joanna Penn for The Creative Penn. Your resources helped me start my journey as an indie author, and your blog and podcast continue to be a big help as I make my way. Mom, Dad and all the family who by blood or choice I'm grateful to have for putting up with my willfulness, my relocating thousands of miles away, and my steadfast belief in things that no one else can see. Above all, thanks to my Chief Reader, for your kind heart and your tough feedback, and to my son for all the naps on my back while I drafted and edited.

ABOUT THE AUTHOR

Globetrotter, homebrewer and writer Anthony St. Clair has walked with hairy coos in the Scottish Highlands, choked on seafood in Australia, and watched the full moon rise over Mt. Everest in Tibet. Anthony's travels have also taken him around the sights and beers of Thailand, Japan, India, Canada, Ireland, the USA, Cambodia, China and Nepal. He and his wife live in Oregon and gave their son a passport for his first birthday. Learn more and connect:

www.anthonystclair.com

www.ingramcontent.com/pod-product-compliance
Lightning Source LLC
Chambersburg PA
CBHW061500210726
48287CB00007B/2591